Lavi The Lion
Finds His Pride

story by
Linda Dickerson

illustrations by
Jennifer Rempel

Lavi the Lion Finds His Pride
Copyright © 2005 by Western Pennsylvania School for Blind Children.

Story by Linda Dickerson.
Illustrations by Jennifer Rempel.

Published by
Towers Maguire Publishing, an imprint of The Local History Company

112 North Woodland Road
Pittsburgh, PA 15232-2849
www.TowersMaguire.com
Info@TowersMaguire.com

The names "Towers Maguire Publishing", "The Local History Company", "Publishers of History and Heritage", and their logos are trademarks of The Local History Company.

Special thanks to Nancy Alberts, Mildred Flaherty, and Buster Maxwell who helped enliven Lavi's adventures.
Book design by Navta Associates.

A Braille version of the text is available from the

Western Pennsylvania School for Blind Children
201 North Bellefield Avenue
Pittsburgh, PA 15213

ISBN-13: 978-0-9744715-2-5
ISBN-10: 0-9744715-2-6

Library of Congress Cataloging-in-Publication Data
Dickerson, Linda, 1961-
    Lavi the Lion Finds His Pride / story by Linda Dickerson ; illustrations by Jennifer Rempel.
        p. cm.
    ISBN 0-9744715-2-6 (alk. paper)
    I. Rempel, Jennifer, ill. II. Title.
    PZ7.D5573Lav 2005
    [E]--dc22
                                            2004026563
Printed in Korea.

ACKNOWLEDGMENTS

There are many people who worked diligently to make this book a reality: Linda Dickerson for telling Lavi's story and donating it to the School; Jennifer Rempel who brought Lavi alive in character; and especially Bernita Buncher and the Buncher Foundation for their strong commitment to making the world a better place for children.

This book is dedicated to the magic of childhood and to the concept that all children—those with disabilities and those without—enjoy an imaginative tale.

Janet Simon, PhD
Executive Director
Western Pennsylvania School for Blind Children

A lion family is called a pride. When a male lion is
no longer a cub, he leaves to roam on his own.

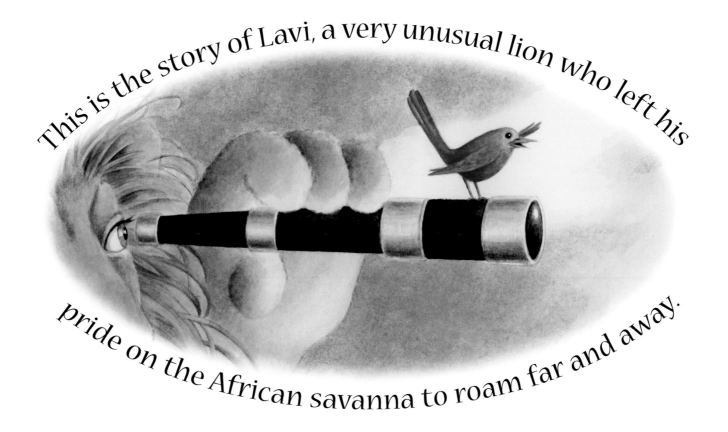

This is the story of Lavi, a very unusual lion who left his
pride on the African savanna to roam far and away.

Join him as he travels the world because, as you will find out …

Lavi was the most adventurous lion on the savanna.

I'm too old to live here with mom and the cubs—

I'm bored! I'm going to find a new pride in a place I've never been before.

Lavi grabbed a flight to a place he had always wanted to see... Katmandu.

There must be lots of big cats in KATmandu, he thought.

Landing in
Katmandu, Lavi
climbed to the top of Mount
Everest, one of the tallest mountains
in the world. He peered through his lion-
locating telescope, turning in all directions. Still
no big cats. Lavi huffed, "They should call this
place NO-KATmandu."

"OK," he said, "I will just keep searching."

Grabbing his extra large lion parachute from his suitcase,

Lavi leapt into midair, and floated all the way to Rome, Italy and into the ruins of the Roman Coliseum.

"Whoa! This is some place."

Lavi listened to a tour guide explain that a long time ago, the Roman emperors would throw their enemies into the Coliseum to fight hungry lions.

"Yikes! I like people, but not for lunch."

Lavi liked music and cowboys so he decided to try Austin, Texas.

It was hot—sort of like being on the savanna. He didn't see any big cats, but he found a band of "cool cats." The band heard his ROARRR, and asked him to be their lead singer.

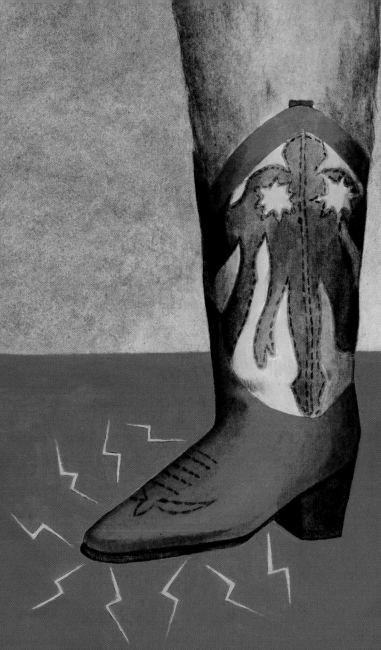

Lavi was a
hit, but his
big paws
hurt from
squeezing
into those
skinny
cowboy
boots!

He decided it was time to keep searching.

Lavi liked all the traveling and adventure, but he wanted to find a pride of his own. He sat in the Austin airport and stared at a map.

"Where are you headed, Mr. Lion?" a businessman asked Lavi.

"I'm looking for a new home," said Lavi, "and I can't find a place I really like."

"Maybe you should visit Pittsburgh. That's where I live. We've got lots of fun activities—museums, sports, music—and great views. You'll love our Pittsburgh Pride. It's everywhere."

Lavi jumped up. "Pittsburgh Pride! That's for me!"

And he caught the next plane to Pittsburgh, Pennsylvania.

Lavi raced up to the lookout on Mount Washington.

STEELERS
vs LIONS!

He saw lots of
tall buildings.

He saw three rivers
coming together at a
point with a big fountain.

On the north shore, he saw a stadium
and a sign: "Steelers versus Lions!"

Lavi rushed to
the incline
rail car station.

"One ticket to get over to those lions, please."

The ticket seller chuckled. "Those aren't real lions. They are
a football team from Detroit. Go to the zoo and you will find lions."

"**Finally! Lions!**" Lavi shouted.

Lavi was in too much of a
hurry to wait for the incline.
He slid all the way down the
mountain on the incline tracks...

Sprinted across a bridge...

Raced past every car on the parkway...

And followed the signs to the zoo where he found the lion's den.

ZOO

"I'm Lavi from Africa, and I am searching for a new pride. Are you the Pittsburgh Pride?"

The big male lion smiled, "Well, yes, we are."

"But, I'm sorry Lavi,
we have a full house!"

Lavi wandered sadly around the city
until he stumbled upon the Carnegie
Museum of Natural History.
Being a curious cat, he trotted in...

and skidded to a halt.

He was staring up into
the sharp teeth of a
tyrannosaurus rex.

Whew! It was just a bunch of bones.

But wait… what is wrong with these lions?

A little girl tugged on his tail.

"Excuse me, Mr. Lion, but the only lions here are stuffed!"

Lavi ran outside.

I feel awful! How will I ever find my pride!

He sat down on a bench and rested his head in his furry paws.

Suddenly, he heard children laughing. Cubs!
He missed romping with the cubs.

WESTERN PENNSYLVANIA
SCHOOL FOR
BLIND CHILDREN

When he looked over the fence,
he saw a place called the Western
Pennsylvania School For Blind Children.

Lavi walked in. "I need some help."

"That's what we do here!" exclaimed the lady at the desk. "We help!"

Lavi asked her about Pittsburgh Pride and she laughed. "Oh that's not a lion pride. It means that Pittsburghers take pride in their city."

"Come and meet the children, our own pride."

"What a nice group of human cubs you are." Children crowded around Lavi.

Soon he was telling stories of his adventures from Africa to Pittsburgh.

When Lavi finished his story, all the children clapped.

One little boy whispered in Lavi's ear. "Please stay with us."

Lavi roared. "Yes, I would love to stay with you!"

"You can be our mane man!" said the little boy.

"Yea!" shouted the children, giving him a big lion hug.

Lavi looked around at all the friendly faces as he rubbed heads with his new friends.

Lavi moaned with happiness.

"You may not be lions, but you are my pride and joy."

Everybody at the school loved Lavi so much that they installed a big heated rock for him just so he would not get cold in the winter.

Lavi had a new home.

Lavi had found his Pittsburgh pride.

Fun Lion Facts! Courtesy of the Pittsburgh Zoo and PPG Aquarium

Size: Male lions in the wild weigh over 400 pounds. Females are smaller and usually weigh less than 300 pounds. The male develops his lush mane at about three years and it reaches maximum development at around five years.

Babies and Young Lions: Lion cubs weigh only two to four and one-half pounds at birth and are as helpless as newborn kittens. They are dependent on the pride for food until about 16 months. Young males leave the pride to roam on their own when they are about two and one-half years old.

Location and habitat: Lions are native to the savanna and plains of Sub-Saharan Africa.

Living arrangements: Female lions live in prides that may include young males. Resident males gain control of a pride territory in competition with other males. Pride size varies from a few lions to as many as 40.

Communication: A lion's roar can be heard for up to five miles and is used to maintain contact with the pride and to intimidate rivals.

Male lions strut as a display of dominance, mainly to impress females.

Lions greet each other by moaning softly and leaning so heavily on one another that one often falls over! They also rub heads to say hello.

Lions moan when they're happy, just like cats purr.

Food: Lions hunt in groups and also scavenge prey killed by other predators. The female lion is the main hunter. The males only hunt if no female brings them food, or if there is nothing to scavenge.

Paws: Real lions have five toes on each of their front feet and four toes on each of their back feet. Like most cats, they have special claws that pull into their footpads rather than remaining out all the time.

Vests: Real lions don't wear vests.

Did you know that the Pittsburgh Zoo has a heated rock for its lions? It's just like Lavi's rock!

More animal facts: A group of lions is a pride, but what are these other groups of animals called?

Cattle   **Whales**   **Birds and sheep**   **Geese**

Can you name other groups of animals?

Answers: A herd of cattle, a pod of whales, a flock of birds or sheep, a gaggle of geese.

ORDER ADDITIONAL COPIES OF
LAVI THE LION FINDS HIS PRIDE

by *LINDA DICKERSON* with illustrations by *JENNIFER REMPEL*
(ISBN 0-9744715-2-6)

from TOWERS MAGUIRE PUBLISHING

(an imprint of THE LOCAL HISTORY COMPANY*)*

ORDER FORM—PLEASE PRINT CLEARLY

NAME _____

COMPANY (if applicable) _____

ADDRESS _____

CITY _____ STATE _____ ZIP _____

PHONE _____ We require your phone number so we can contact you in case there is a problem with your order. Your privacy is important to us: We do not sell or trade your personal information with others.

Please allow 2-4 weeks for delivery. Prices subject to change without notice. All book sales are final. US shipments only (contact us for information on international orders). Payable by check, money order, or Visa/MasterCard in US funds (no cash orders accepted).

PLEASE SEND _____ copies at $15.95 each .... Subtotal:　　$_____

Sales Tax: PA residents (outside Allegheny County) add 6% per copy

　　　　　　　　Allegheny County, PA residents add 7% per copy　　　　$_____

Add $5 shipping/packaging for the first copy and $1 each additional copy　　$_____

　　　　　　　　　　　　　　　　TOTAL AMOUNT DUE:　　$_____

PAYMENT BY CHECK/MONEY ORDER:

___ Enclosed is my check/money order for the total amount due made payable to: *Towers Maguire Publishing.*

PAYMENT BY VISA OR MASTERCARD Credit Card:

Bill my ____ Visa ____ MasterCard Account # _____
(Address above must be the same as on file with your credit card company)

Expires _____ Name as it appears on your card _____

　　　　　Signature _____

Mail or Fax your order to:　Towers Maguire Publishing　　www.TowersMaguire.com
　　　　　　　　　　　　　　The Local History Company　　Sales@TowersMaguire.com
　　　　　　　　　　　　　　112 NORTH Woodland Road　　(FAX 412-362-8192)
　　　　　　　　　　　　　　Pittsburgh, PA 15232-2849

　　　　　　　　　　　　　　Or—Call 412-362-2294 with your order.